To Laura

ISBN 0-439-58439-6

12 11 10 9 8 7 6 5 4 3 2 1   3 4 5 6 7 8/0

Printed in Mexico   49

First Scholastic printing, September 2003

The artist used pencil on watercolor paper to create the illustrations for this book.

Designed by Martha Rago

Hondo & Fabian

written and illustrated by

Peter McCarty

SCHOLASTIC INC.
New York Toronto London Auckland Sydney
Mexico City New Delhi Hong Kong Buenos Aires

Fabian on the windowsill,
Hondo on the floor—
two sleepy pets
in their favorite places.

"Wake up, Hondo.

Time to go!"

Hondo will have an adventure.

Fabian will stay home.

Where is Hondo going,
riding in a car?

Hondo is going to the beach
to meet his friend Fred.

Fabian is going to
the living room
to play with the baby.

Two happy dogs
dive in the waves.

Fabian dives for the door.

Hondo has fun with Fred.

Fabian has fun too.

Now Hondo is getting hungry.

He wishes he could eat the fish.

Fabian is getting hungry too.

He wishes he could eat

the turkey sandwich.

At last Hondo comes home.
It's time for dinner!

Side by side Hondo and Fabian

eat their food.

Hondo and Fabian, full and fat—
in their favorite places once again.

"Good night, Hondo."
"Good night, Fabian."

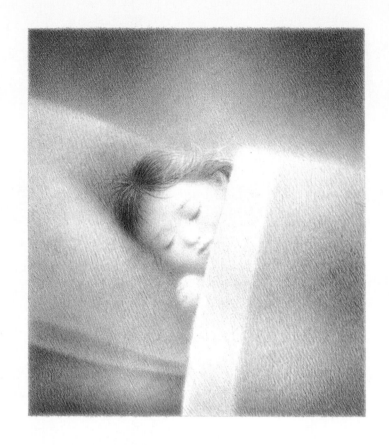

"Good night, baby!"